SURYA

AND THE ZERO POINT CONSPIRACY

SURYA

AND THE ZERO POINT CONSPIRACY

Dr. Prabhat Bhattacharyya

Translated by

Partha Mukhopadhyay

EXCELLER BOOKS®
A GLOBAL PRESS

Surya and the Zero Point Conspiracy

Cover by Exceller Books
Translated by Partha Mukhopadhyay

ISBN: 978-93-47397-50-9

Published in India in 2025 by Exceller Books,
An imprint of GE Group,
G1, Dream Apartment, Degree College Road, Belgharia,
Kolkata, 700056, India
www.excellerbooks.com

EXCELLER BOOKS®
A GLOBAL PRESS

Dedicated to my family, teachers and patients

Krishna had come for a photography assignment at a cultural program. Once the assignment was done, he was about to head home when his phone rang.

"Hello, didi,"He smiled and answered.

"What's going on with you?"

"Everything is fine here. How are you? You haven't visited in a long time."

"I'll come today. Christmas is only a few days away. Why don't we go somewhere for a bit?"

"That's a wonderful idea! I'll tell dada."

"Alright. I'll talk to him again in the afternoon."

"Okay."

Krishna quickly left for home. Not long after he arrived, Surya returned as well.

"You had an assignment today, didn't you?" Surya asked.

"Yes, I'll show you everything. Ujjayini didi had called."

"She called me too. She might come over later. She mentioned going on a trip."

"Yes, that would be great."

Who does not enjoy travelling? They had visited many places across the country and abroad for investigative work.

After a while, the doorbell rang. Ujjayini had arrived.

"I baked a cake and brought it for you."

"That's wonderful. It looks fantastic." Krishna went to fetch a knife.

As they ate the cake, they began planning a short getaway.

"We should go somewhere, but not too far," Surya suggested.

"A friend of mine recently visited Jhargram. They loved it. I'm thinking of going there," said Ujjayini.

"I've heard Jhargram is really beautiful," Krishna added.

"Alright then, let's go to Jhargram. We'll need to make the arrangements," said Surya.

"I'll handle that. Some of my friends stayed at Somani Resorts. It's a very nice place. I'll book it for us," Krishna said.

"Well, my cousin Aishika lives in Raipur and has come to Kolkata to visit. She will join us too," said Ujjayini.

Krishna nodded. "Sure, there's no problem."

"Then we can take our car," Surya said, glancing at Krishna with a smile.

"I'll drive for a bit, too," Ujjayini chimed in.

Everything was set, and the journey began on the morning of December 25th.

• • •

The road was quite beautiful, and they stopped for breakfast along the way.

"I just got a call from Somani Resort. They wanted to know what we'd like for lunch," Ujjayini informed them.

Within a few hours, they reached the resort. It was very pleasant. One double room was allotted to Surya and Krishna, and another to Ujjayini and Aishika.

"Let's go out after lunch," Ujjayini suggested.

"So be it," Surya agreed.

Abhishek Somani, the owner's son, was at the reception. Since his father was ill, he was handling everything. Krishna had already gathered all the necessary information. Their pet Alsatian was tied nearby.

"Oh, I'm scared just looking at him," Aishika said.

"Hey, are you afraid of dogs?" Abhishek asked with a smile.

Lunch was quite good. After eating, they set out again.

"I'll drive for a bit," Ujjayini said, settling into the driver's seat.

Abhishek had told them what places they could visit, and they already knew a little about them. Jhargram, in Medinipur, is a famous place with a large tribal population. Their first stop was Jhargram Rajbari, but they couldn't go inside as entry was strictly prohibited. The palace has now been converted into a hotel. They stepped inside the gate, admired the exterior, and took photographs.

"Very beautiful," Krishna remarked.

A brief history was written on a plaque outside. Ujjayini had already read some of it. She began, "This is the Jhargram Palace. It was founded by Raja Sarveshwar Singh in the 16th century. He came with his elder brother to conquer this region. They had been sent by Raja Man Singh of Amer, whom Emperor Akbar had appointed as the subahdar of Bengal, Bihar, and Orissa. After defeating the local tribal chiefs,

Sarveshwar Singh established this place and named it Jhargram, which means a village surrounded by forests. Earlier, the area was called Jangalkhand. The rulers here bore the title of Malladeva. However, the British never recognized it as an independent kingdom."

"Wow, that was a beautiful history lesson!" Krishna exclaimed.

Next, they drove through the forest to see the Kanakdurga Temple.

"It feels really nice here," Aishika said.

"There are so many kinds of trees," Krishna added.

"Beware of monkeys," Surya warned.

The old temple was dilapidated, with a large crack running through its centre. It was said that lightning had struck it. The door was closed, and the old idol was visible through the crack. The new temple stood on the opposite side, well preserved.

"There used to be a golden idol here," Ujjayini said.

Nearby, the narrow but beautiful Dulung River flowed gently. They took many pictures there.

Then they went to see the Chilkigarh Palace. On one side of the river stood the Kanakdurga Temple, and on the other, the old palace.

"Dulung is a small tributary of the Subarnarekha," Surya informed them.

The Chilkigarh Palace was founded in the thirteenth century by King Jagannath Dhabaldev. He built the palace-fort on the riverbank to defend against Bargi attacks. Legend says the goddess Mahamaya appeared in his dream and instructed him to create an idol of her. He then built the idol and the

Kanakdurga Temple. The palace was now in ruins, and everyone wandered around in silence.

On one side, a house had completely collapsed. Krishna peered inside. As he turned, he suddenly saw a man lying motionless on the ground. A knife was lodged in his chest, and blood was oozing out.

Startled, he ran to call Surya.

"Hey, what happened? Why are you running?" Surya asked.

"Please come with me. You'll understand when you see it."

Surya followed him back.

"Hey, where did the body go?" Krishna said in shock.

"What body?"

"I saw a man lying there with a knife in his chest. And now he's gone!"

"Are you sure you didn't imagine it?"

"Why would I make such a huge mistake?"

"Okay, let's look around."

They searched thoroughly but found nothing.

"There are bloodstains, though," Surya said. "Right where you said you saw him."

"That means I really did see someone murdered. And by the time I came back, the body was not there."

"That seems likely. You check over there; I'll look around this side. Okay?"

"Alright."

After a while, Surya called out to Krishna and said, "Come on, they must be looking for us. There's no need to tell anyone anything right now."

"You're right."

As they emerged from the rubble, they ran into Ujjayini and Aishika.

"Where were you two? I've been looking for you for so long. I left my phone at the hotel," Ujjayini said.

"I was over there," Krishna said, pointing at the spot.

Since it was getting dark, they decided to return. On the way, Surya asked a shopkeeper where the police station was.

"What will you do at the police station?" Ujjayini asked.

"I have a friend there. I'll just meet him."

Surya went inside the station alone. He introduced himself to the officer and briefly explained what had happened.

"Alright, I'll go check it out," Officer Sujoybabu said.

"We'll talk later."

"Okay."

Without further delay, they returned to the hotel.

Back at the resort, they saw the Alsatian tied in the open courtyard. Krishna asked the hotel staff to take him away. Chairs and tables were arranged outside. Over tea and pakoras, they began chatting.

"How was the tour?" Abhishek asked.

"We had a great time," Surya replied.

"I liked the Dulung River the most," Aishika said.

"The river is really beautiful. There must be much more water during the rainy season," Ujjayini added.

"Of course," Abhishek nodded.

"Where can we go tomorrow?" Krishna asked.

"Let's get up early and visit Gopiballavpur. It's a very beautiful place, full of old temples and natural beauty," Ujjayini suggested.

"Alright, let's go there," Surya agreed.

After dinner, they went inside.

"Dinner was excellent," Surya said.

"That's right. So, did you report the matter to the police?" Krishna asked.

"Yes, I did."

"What did they say?"

"They said they would go and investigate."

"Murder here, too! A crime!"

"You don't have to worry. Just focus on enjoying the trip."

"You're right."

They slept well that night.

• • •

After waking up and finishing their morning tea, they prepared to leave for Gopiballavpur. But just as they were about to get into the car, two men appeared and blocked their way. Each held a long knife glinting in the early light. One of them glared at Surya and said, voice low and threatening, "It's not wise to poke your nose into everything. You came here for a tour—keep it that way. Otherwise, you won't go back alive. And hand over that mobile phone you found."

Surya did not bother replying. Instead, he moved—lightning-fast, in perfect sync with Krishna. In an instant, the knives clattered to the ground. The attackers stumbled back and fled, disappearing around the corner.

Abhishek rushed over. "What happened!" he asked, panic rising in his voice.

"A small matter. Nothing to worry about," Surya said, brushing it off.

"No, this is serious. We should inform the police."

"Alright, I'll call them on the way. No need to panic so much."

"What's going on?" Ujjayini asked, sensing the tension.

"I'll explain everything once we start."

Krishna started the car, and Surya narrated everything. When he finished, Ujjayini sighed, "Here too—another incident. Bloodshed in the palace."

"Well, you said it yourself—bloodshed in the palace," Krishna replied. "Does that scare you?" Surya asked.

"Do we look timid?" Aishika shot back. "Honestly, it feels thrilling—like we're part of some mysterious expedition."

"That's the spirit," Krishna said with a grin.

Surya called Sujoybabu and reported the attack.

"This is complicated," Sujoybabu said gravely. "We went there yesterday and found nothing—no one, no traces except blood stains. We'll look into it. Meanwhile, be extremely careful."

"Don't worry. We'll talk later," Surya said and ended the call.

Then he reached into his pocket and pulled out a gun. "I've got this, too. You don't need to be worried about your safety."

"Wonderful! Can I try it?" Aishika asked eagerly.

"Sure. But be careful," Surya said, handing her the weapon.

"I have one as well," Krishna added casually.

"Then our safety just doubled," Ujjayini said.

"Abhishek was looking pale and uneasy," Krishna said.

"That's quite natural," Surya told him.

Breakfast arrived soon after.

"I took pictures of those two men," Ujjayini said.

"Excellent. Send them to me—I'll forward them to the officer. Let's see if they can track them down," Surya said.

Within moments, the photos were on Sujoybabu's phone.

"Good. Don't worry—they'll be arrested soon," he replied.

"Those men mentioned a mobile phone," Krishna said. "What was that about?"

"Who knows," Surya said, shrugging, unconcerned.

By the time they reached Gopiballavpur, the tension faded. The place was breathtaking—set along the banks of the Subarnarekha River, shimmering in the sunlight. Surya remembered reading about it online. Once called Kashipur, the region later took its name from Gopiballav, another name for Lord Krishna. Temples, forests, old ruins—Gopiballavpur held them all.

The river was shallow, its sands glittering.

"Tell me why this river is called Subarnarekha," Ujjayini asked.

"I know that," Krishna said confidently. "The sand sparkles like gold—hence the name."

"Correct. It looks like someone has done their homework," Ujjayini teased.

"It's said this place is connected to the Ramayana," Surya added. "Legend says the robber Ratnakar roamed these forests before becoming sage Valmiki. His Tapovan Ashram was here. Sita lived here with her sons, Luv and Kush. People believe Valmiki wrote the Ramayana sitting in front of the Rameshwar temple."

"Fascinating," Aishika said.

They explored the area. Many temples were in ruins, but still mesmerizing.

"It is said that Sita's footprints can be found here," Ujjayini whispered.

"And where's this Rameshwar temple?" Krishna asked, scanning the surroundings.

"Stay alert," Surya cautioned everyone.

"Okay."

"Come on, let's find a place for lunch," he said.

On their way back, Ujjayini and Aishika broke into song, their voices drifting over the countryside. The visit to Gopiballavpur ended smoothly—almost too smoothly for a day that had begun with knives.

• • •

As soon as they stepped back into the hotel lobby, Abhishek hurried over. "I hope everything went smoothly, right?"

"No, no—everything was fine. We had a great trip," Krishna replied.

"I was worrying for nothing," Abhishek heaved a sigh of relief.

After a quick coffee, everyone retreated to their rooms. Before heading to their room, Surya asked Abhishek for a room on the second floor.

"No problem," Abhishek said with a reassuring smile, "The one upstairs is vacant. I'll arrange it right away."

Since everyone was tired, they quickly finished dinner and went to bed.

"It's oddly quiet around here," Krishna murmured.

"So I noticed."

Saying this, Surya switched on the TV, sat down and started watching it.

• • •

A sudden noise snapped Krishna awake in the dead of night. Blinking against the darkness, he noticed Surya on the balcony, pistol clenched tightly in his hand.

"They tried to break the door," Surya said, his voice low but steady. "Ran the moment I fired."

From the balcony below, the Alsatian's frantic howling cut through the silence.

Within moments, the alarm bell shrieked, and Ujjayini, Aishika, and Abhishek rushed out, faces pale.

"They bolted the second they saw the gun," Abhishek said breathlessly. "But why are they so furious with you?"

"I'll explain later," Surya replied. "I don't think they'll return tonight. Now, let's go to sleep."

They all dispersed, worry etched across their faces.

Krishna lay awake, thoughts spinning, until exhaustion finally pulled him under.

When Krishna woke up in the morning, he saw Surya standing on the veranda. Seeing him, he said, "A new day, new hope. Let's hold on to the light."

Over breakfast, Surya turned to Abhishek. "We're heading back to Kolkata today. We've troubled you enough."

"Not at all. But… what's going on?"

"I'll tell you everything later. I have your number."

"Okay, dada."

Their first stop was the police station. Surya went inside and talked to Sujoybabu.

"Did you go there yesterday?" Surya asked.

"I did. But the place was empty— they had flown. Still, I followed your lead and found the white powder. I sent it for forensic testing," Sujoybabu said.

Surya recounted the previous night's attack.

"So they're still active," Sujoybabu murmured, suspicion glinting in his eyes. "You were right. A big gang is involved."

"We're returning to Kolkata today, but we'll stay in touch," Surya said.

"Of course." Sujoybabu shook his hand firmly.

From there, they stopped at an art hub brimming with striking paintings, masks, and sculptures. One particular mask caught Krishna's eye, and he bought it immediately.

"Good choice," Surya said with a faint smile.

Krishna, a mask enthusiast, had a collection of masks from various places. Ujjayini and Aishika bought some beautiful paintings.

"You have wonderful pieces here," Krishna told the shop owner.

"We have a branch in Kolkata as well," the owner said, handing him a card.

"Let's move," Surya said.

Next, they visited the famous Jhargram Deer Park.

"Those are *neel gais*," Aishika pointed out.

"They appeared the moment we arrived," Ujjayini noted.

"They're probably hungry." Krishna crouched down, tearing a handful of grass and offering it through the net. The deer devoured it eagerly, and soon everyone joined in feeding them.

With that, their trip to Jhargram came to an end.

"I kept my eyes open the whole time. Didn't spot anything strange," Krishna said.

"Good. Let's head home," Surya replied.

As they drove back, Surya muttered, "It's not good to be involved in all this."

"Not at all—I enjoyed the thrill," Aishika said with a grin.

• • •

After returning to Kolkata, Krishna said, "So now we have to solve the mystery of the 'bloodshed in the palace.' This should be easy for you. I'm sure you've already made plenty of progress."

"It's not that simple," Surya replied quietly.

Just then, Surya's phone rang. It was Sujoybabu.

"You were right," Sujoybabu said without preamble. "A body has been found in a paddy field near Chilkigarh Rajbari—stab wound to the chest. It's been sent for postmortem."

"Alright," Surya said, ending the call.

Krishna raised an eyebrow. "So I did see it correctly."

"Do you ever make a mistake?" Surya muttered.

Later, Surya visited the detective department. What he heard there confirmed his instincts—the matter was not confined to a single location. The trail was spreading, but they were determined to chase it down to the very end.

That night, Krishna asked, "Why was the man killed? Can you figure out the motive?"

"No. Nothing makes sense yet," Surya admitted.

"It could be about a hidden treasure," Krishna said. "In a palace like that, anything could be buried. Maybe that's what all this trouble is about."

"Maybe you're right," Surya said with a tired yawn, before finally drifting off to sleep.

• • •

It was a Saturday evening. Surya was driving his car with Pankaj Sarkar, an expert officer from the Detective Department, beside him. Speeding along the bypass, they went past Ruby and headed towards Garia. Eventually, they stopped at a secluded place in Garia.

"Is this the place?" Surya asked.

"Yes, this is the place. Let's go," Pankaj replied.

There was a dilapidated house with its door hanging open as if waiting for them.

With four armed policemen following close behind, they stepped inside.

"No one's here. They've all fled," Pankaj muttered.

"Looks like they got wind of our arrival and cleared out early," Surya said.

"Could be," Pankaj agreed.

"Check that corner," Surya instructed, striding forward.

There, sprawled motionless on the cold floor, was the body of a tall foreigner.

"Looks like they killed him and abandoned the place," Pankaj said grimly.

"We need to search for anything they might have left behind," Surya said.

Suddenly, Surya noticed something and said, "Wait—what's this? A time bomb. Thirty seconds left. Move! Everyone, out!"

They bolted from the house, sprinting until they were a safe distance away.

A thunderous explosion tore through the night.

Shaken but steadying himself, Pankaj immediately called the fire brigade and the forensics team.

"Good thing you spotted it. We'd be in pieces by now," he said.

"They wanted to erase everything—including us. They must have known exactly when we'd show up," Surya said.

Soon, fire brigade units and forensic teams flooded the scene.

Once the chaos had settled, Surya turned and walked back toward what remained of the house.

• • •

When Surya finally returned home, Krishna frowned. "Why are you so late today? And why do you look so exhausted?"

Without saying anything, Surya simply lowered himself onto the sofa.

"Fine," Krishna sighed. "Have some tea and try to relax."

That night, as Surya lay staring at the ceiling, his thoughts churned. *I came back from the edge of death today. The enemy is far more dangerous than I imagined. I'll have to move very carefully.*

The next morning, he made a brief call. "Alright, Raja, that's it then," he said before hanging up. Soon after, he stepped out, and while waiting near the Maniktala bus stand, his phone buzzed. It was Raja.

"Sir, I'm coming," he said.

Within minutes, Raja appeared, and the two went into a nearby restaurant. Surya ordered tea and an omelette, and then started the conversation. "Raja, can you handle the job?"

"I'm here for you, sir. Tell me where to go."

"Diamond Harbour. I need information—details that only you can get. I'll explain everything."

Raja nodded. "Once I have it, I'll inform you."

"But you'll have to be extremely careful. No one should suspect anything."

"You can trust me," Raja said firmly.

"Good. That's all for now. I'll contact you later."

After finishing their food, they rose to leave.

Surya slipped some money into Raja's hand, and Raja accepted it quietly. He was Surya's most trusted and reliable informer. Surya once saved him from a big danger, and that made him loyal to Surya.

• • •

Returning home, Surya found Ujjayini seated with Krishna, deep in conversation.

"So, sir... how far has the investigation progressed?" Ujjayini asked, eyes sharp with curiosity.

"Not very far," Surya replied. His gaze shifted to the table. "What's in that packet?"

"Makha Sandesh," Ujjayini said.

"Excellent," Surya said, his expression brightening.

"I really liked Jhargram," Ujjayini continued. "I hope we get another trip like that."

"Let's hope so," Surya agreed.

"Why don't we go to Purulia this time?" Krishna suggested.

"It's a beautiful place," Ujjayini added. "Alright, I'll handle all the arrangements."

Their conversation drifted on, time slipping away unnoticed.

• • •

Two days later, Raja called. "Sir, I've located their meeting place."

"Good. I'm on my way. Keep in touch with me," Surya said.

"Yes, sir," Raja replied.

Surya immediately rang Pankaj.

"I'll meet you on the road," Pankaj said.

Surya turned to Krishna. "Do you have any important work today?"

"Are we going to Diamond Harbour?" Krishna asked.

"Yes."

"But why?"

"It's urgent. Just tell me whether you're coming or not."

"I'll go. Wherever you say, I'll go."

"Good."

Surya's car met Pankaj's on the highway, and the two vehicles moved in tandem. Surya then called Raja again, confirmed his location, and picked him up.

"We're entering Diamond Harbour," Pankaj announced.

"This is the place," Raja said, pointing to a nondescript building.

Pankaj and the officers accompanying Surya were all dressed in plain white. Krishna felt a surge of excitement as the operation tightened around them.

"We'll wait and watch. Let's see who goes in or out," Surya instructed.

Minutes crawled by before a lone man appeared. He knocked once, and someone from inside unlatched the door.

Just as he stepped forward, Surya, Pankaj, and Krishna closed in, grabbing both men before they could react. The sight of firearms froze them in place. Except for the two, the entire ground floor was empty.

Leaving the suspects with the police, the trio climbed the stairs. No one was there, but the room contained several items clearly valuable to the investigation.

"Let's move," Surya said at last.

They regrouped outside.

"Operation successful," Pankaj remarked.

"Now, let's interrogate them and see what we can find," Surya said. "But we have to keep a close watch on this house."

• • •

After returning home, Surya asked Krishna, "So, how was the adventure?"

"Great—but I couldn't understand everything," Krishna admitted.

"Don't worry, everything will gradually be clear," Surya assured him.

The next afternoon, after a call from Pankaj, Surya went to his office. They spoke for a few minutes before Surya said, "The picture is slowly getting clearer."

"I may need to go to Lucknow soon," Pankaj replied.

"All right. If needed, I'll go with you. I'll keep you updated," Surya said.

"Of course," Pankaj nodded.

Surya stood to leave, but the moment he stepped outside, someone slammed into him. It wasn't an accident—he felt the deliberate shove—but he managed to keep his balance.

"There's still time. Stay out of this," the man warned before disappearing into the crowd.

Surya steadied himself, murmuring, "So the enemy is getting desperate... trying to scare me off. But retreat isn't something I know. I'll just have to be more careful."

He did not mention the incident to Krishna when he returned home.

A short while later, Ujjayini called. "Everything is arranged for our trip to Purulia. We leave the day after tomorrow."

"Good," Surya said. The break was exactly what he needed.

"All set—no issues. Early morning departure," Ujjayini added. "And Aishika will be joining us."

"Fine," Surya replied.

When Krishna heard, he was delighted.

"I just hope we can travel peacefully this time—no trouble," Surya said, though a part of him knew trouble was already on their trail.

• • •

It took nearly seven hours to reach Purulia, with Krishna and Ujjayini taking turns at the wheel. The wilderness of Purulia unfolded around them—rugged hills, dense forests, and winding rivers that seemed to whisper old secrets.

Their hotel at Baghmundi, beyond the Ayodhya Hills, was large, tastefully decorated, and eerily quiet. By the time they settled down for food and drinks, the late-afternoon sun had already begun to fade behind the hills.

After a brief rest, they headed out to Khayrabera Dam.

"Beautiful place," Surya murmured, watching the last sliver of sunlight melt into the reservoir. They clicked photos against the burning sky before getting back into the car.

"Where are we going now?" Aishika asked.

"Charida Village," Surya replied.

"What's special there?"

"Masks," Ujjayini answered. "The famous Purulia Chhau masks."

Charida was alive with colour—rows of mask shops, each more striking than the last. They wandered from one artisan's stall to another, lost in the craftsmanship. Everyone bought souvenirs; Krishna bought the most.

"Your collection keeps growing," Ujjayini teased.

Surya examined a hand-painted mask closely. "Their craft is extraordinary. But it's time to head back."

"I would like to have a strong cup of tea," Krishna said.

"And maybe a plate of fish fry," Ujjayini added with a smile.

"Just a little more patience," Surya said.

The next day was reserved for the Ayodhya hills—dams, falls, and everything in between. They visited Turga Dam and Turga Falls first, then the Upper and Lower Dams. At Bamni Falls, the long descent was worth every step. The waterfall looked almost unreal, like a painting come alive. Photos were taken, jokes exchanged, and the air felt lighter.

From there, they moved on to Muruguma Dam, and then stopped at a quiet spot for lunch.

"The aloo-posto is amazing," Krishna declared.

"I'm sticking with the fried fish," said Aishika.

Afterwards, they explored Mayur Pahar and Pakhi Pahar—Muraburu Pahar in local terms—where artists had painted vibrant images of birds and animals across the mountain face.

"Incredible," Ujjayini whispered.

Krishna studied each painting as if decoding a hidden message.

Evening crept up on them unnoticed. Back at the hotel, they gathered again to talk. Surya stepped aside to call Pankajbabu.

"Any trouble there?" Pankajbabu asked.

"No, everything is fine," Surya replied.

"Good. Stay alert. Our work here is moving. And, Surya—you'll need to go to Lucknow."

"Understood."

As soon as he returned, Ujjayini said softly, "Nothing's gone wrong so far."

"Let's hope it stays that way," Surya said.

On their way back to Kolkata the next day, they planned quick stops at Jaychandi Hills and Garh Panchakot. Jaychandi Hill demanded a steep climb, but the view from the temple above was worth the effort.

"Everything looks beautiful from up here," Aishika said.

Garh Panchakot followed—a scarred remnant of history at the foot of the Panchet Hills. The ruins whispered stories of the Panchakot kingdom, of rulers, invasions, and time's slow decay. Only the Pancharatna Temple stood with some dignity left.

Krishna wandered through the ruins until Surya's call startled him.

"Thought something strange might happen here, too?" Surya asked lightly.

"No, nothing like that," Krishna said, though his eyes betrayed a flicker of unease.

"You should sketch this place," Surya suggested.

"I will. Look over there," Krishna said, already drawn toward another fragment of history.

"I love these old structures," Ujjayini said.

"They deserve careful restoration," Surya agreed.

Krishna gazed at a broken wall near the hill. "This place feels… different. I've never experienced anything like it."

They had lunch under a tree, on banana leaves, the silence of the ruins settling around them.

And just like that, their Purulia trip came to an end, and it was time to return.

• • •

The next morning, after a brief call with Pankaj, Surya turned to Krishna and said, "Get ready—we're heading to Lucknow."

"Lucknow?" Krishna blinked.

"Yes. We leave tomorrow. Why? Any objections?"

"No, no objections," Krishna replied, though his voice carried suspicion. "I'm happy to travel… but I'm guessing this isn't just a casual trip."

"You're absolutely right," Surya said calmly.

"That's fine then. A little action doesn't hurt. A twist in the tale… some mystery, some thrill—I'm ready."

"Well said. Start packing."

"Alright."

The moment Krishna shared the news with Ujjayini, she sighed. "You two only know how to roam around. Be careful."

"Of course, didi. We'll be cautious," Krishna assured her.

Before leaving, Surya spoke to Pankaj once more.

"If you don't go, nothing will move forward there. That's why I said it," Pankaj insisted. "Sugata Roy will accompany you—sharp guy."

"Good. And if needed, we can rely on the local police, right?" Surya asked.

"Yes. Sugata will make all the arrangements," Pankaj replied.

• • •

Surya, Krishna, and Sugata arrived in Lucknow—a city steeped in age-old traditions, once the pride of Oudh and now the capital of Uttar Pradesh. Its lanes still whispered stories of Akbar's reign, of Nawabs shifting capitals, and of the sparks that ignited the Sepoy Mutiny. But none of that history mattered today. They were here for something far more perilous.

"We have to find the place," Sugata said grimly.

"I already know where it is," Surya replied.

Sugata raised an eyebrow. "Is that so?"

"Yes. Krishna, we'll need disguises this time," Surya said, his voice low.

"So… this is a mission?" Krishna asked.

"That's right. And this time, we can't afford a single mistake. The place we're heading to is extremely dangerous."

Krishna nodded silently.

"I'll coordinate with the local police and bring two or four armed officers," Sugata added.

"Good. We'll need them," Surya agreed.

Soon, Surya, Krishna, Sugata, and four policemen headed out. Surya and Krishna, now in disguise, looked nothing like themselves.

When they reached a crowded street, Surya signalled the driver to stop. He stepped out, scanning the area.

"Krishna and I will go inside that house," Surya instructed. "You stay outside. If things go wrong, I'll call or WhatsApp you."

"Understood," Sugata said.

Surya and Krishna moved toward a small, dilapidated house and rang the bell. A rugged man opened the door, his expression cold.

"What do you want?" he growled.

"Sweets," Surya answered calmly.

"Come in." His voice was rough, almost threatening.

The moment they stepped inside, the door slammed shut behind them. They were escorted into a dim room where a sinister-looking man sat in a chair, flanked by two others. He was clearly the boss.

"Boss, they've come for sweets," the rugged man announced in Hindi.

The boss narrowed his eyes. "Do you know them?"

"No, boss. They just showed up."

"These aren't real people," the boss said, his tone suddenly sharp. "Look at their faces."

Krishna's fake beard was hanging loose.

"They've come with bad intentions. Tie them up," the boss ordered his men, and they advanced toward Surya and Krishna.

"You're making a mistake. We're customers," Surya warned.

"Wrong! Ha ha ha!" the boss bellowed.

His men took hold of Surya's hands.

Just then, the door burst open, and Sugata stormed in with his gun raised, and four policemen following him. Surya had already informed him earlier.

"Hands up!" Sugata commanded.

The boss and his men were immediately subdued. Officers swept through the rooms, uncovering several large packing crates.

"Operation successful," Surya declared. "This is one of their hubs. There's another one somewhere in India."

"Where?" Krishna asked.

"In Bangalore. And their main base is in Bangkok."

"Then we'll have to go there too," Krishna said.

"Absolutely. We're going to shut down every one of their operations," Surya replied, his voice steeled with resolve.

On the way back, Sugata leaned back in the car and said, "You took a massive risk."

Surya grinned. "Sometimes you have to. And besides, you showed up just in time."

"I'm feeling quite good about this," Krishna admitted.

Sugata chuckled. "Bravo—fearless as ever!"

"Thank you. Actually, I needed to tell you something," Krishna said.

"I know," Surya cut in. "You want to explore the city, right?"

"Yes! Exactly," Krishna said with a wide smile.

"That's a great idea," Sugata said. "Tomorrow, we'll properly explore Lucknow. Even I need a break from all this crime."

"Agreed," Surya said.

After dinner, everyone headed home.

Krishna called Ujjayini and recounted the day's events.

"You did well," she said, "but it was dangerous."

"We're touring Lucknow tomorrow," Krishna told her.

"Wow, wonderful! I've visited it before."

"Then you must have gone to Bhulbhulaiyya," Surya said.

"Yes—Bhulbhulaiyya, the Imambara, everything. And bring me a chikan saree."

"Okay," Krishna said.

• • •

The next morning, the journey to Lucknow began. The main attractions of this city are the Imambara and the Bhulbhulaiyya. The Bara Imambara was built by Nawab Asaf-ud-Daula. Its architecture is extraordinary. It is said that it was designed by Kifayat Ullah, a relative of the architect of the Taj Mahal. It has a mix of Mughal and Rajput architecture, as well as Gothic influences.

Far ahead, there is a huge hall with a very high ceiling. It is amazing how skillfully it has been built. Above it is the famous labyrinth, the Bhulbhulaiyya. How many pathways twist this way and that! There is a real fear of getting lost without a guide.

"What darkness!" said Krishna.

"Yes, we should stay together and follow the guide," Surya said. "But whatever you say, it is a great experience."

From there, they went up to the roof.

"The entire city of Lucknow can be seen from here," Sugata said.

"That's the clock tower," the guide pointed out.

Another important feature of the Bara Imambara is the Shahi Baoli, or Shahi Hamam, which is actually a series of steps or stepwells. It is connected to the Gomti River.

The Chhota Imambara was built by Nawab Mohammad Ali Shah. The tombs of the Nawab and his mother are there. Its interior is beautifully decorated, with chandeliers and crystal lamps brought from Belgium. They also visited this place.

Then they visited the British Residency. The houses there were used as the residence of the British Resident General. During the Sepoy Mutiny, there were more than 3,000 British residents in the area.

"The houses are all dilapidated," Krishna said.

Everyone took photos standing in front of the cannon. There is a museum in the square, which they also visited.

They also visited the Clock Tower. It was built in the style of Big Ben in London. Its design resembles a flower with twelve petals.

This time, they visited the Lucknow Zoo, officially called the Nawab Wajid Ali Shah Zoological Garden.

"I really like visiting the zoo," Krishna said.

There is a butterfly park there, along with toy trains and boating facilities. The Lucknow State Museum is located within the premises of this zoo. It houses many ancient artefacts, including a large collection of sculptures. There is also an Egyptian mummy.

After lunch, they went to Aminabad Market.

"Here you can find clothes, jewellery, shoes, carpets, handicrafts, etc. There are also many good places to eat," said the guide.

After shopping, they returned to the hotel with biryani.

• • •

Coming back, Sugata said, "Tomorrow we will leave for Bangalore from here."

"Tomorrow?" Krishna asked.

"Yes, that's right," Surya said. "The sooner we can go, the better."

"Have you noticed one thing? They've placed the real bases in places where there won't be much suspicion," Sugata said.

"Absolutely right," said Surya.

Bangalore is also called Bengaluru. It is the capital of Karnataka. It is a very developed city.

Entering the hotel, Krishna asked, "Is there a new type of work here?"

"Yes." Saying that, Surya called someone.

What he said in Hindi and English meant this: he wanted to do business with those who had come from Kolkata.

Then he said "OK" and hung up the phone.

"What happened?" Krishna asked.

"We have to meet someone at the King's Hotel this evening. Okay, Sugata Babu, we have some work to do."

"What is it?" asked Sugata.

"We need to talk to the police station here and arrange for two armed policemen to accompany us."

"Okay, I'll arrange it."

Sugata made the arrangements, and then they went on an evening expedition.

"I'm not asking any questions," Sugata said with a smile.

A mysterious smile appeared on Surya's face.

As soon as they entered the King's Hotel, the three of them took a table and sat down. Just then, Surya's mobile rang.

Surya picked up the phone and said, "Look to your left."

As soon as the person with the mobile phone looked at him, Surya waved at him.

He and his companion came forward toward them.

"Are you Surya?" he asked.

"Yes, sit down," Surya said.

They spoke in low voices as they sipped coffee and nibbled on snacks. After a while, they stood up, and so did Surya.

Then they walked outside with Surya. Krishna and Sugata followed them.

A car was parked outside, and two very tough-looking men were standing in front of it. As soon as the two came out, they quickly pushed them into the car. Then Sugata told Surya to get in quickly. As soon as they got in, the car started moving.

Sugata, holding a pistol in his hand, said to the two men with whom Surya had been talking, "Be quiet. Look what you have fallen into! Give me your mobile phones." They handed over their mobile phones without any hesitation.

"You handled things well," Surya said to Sugata as the car rolled up to the police station. The two arrested men were taken inside.

"We need to interrogate them and trace the real hideout," Surya added.

Officer-in-Charge Narayan Swamy arrived and introduced himself.

"The trap was laid perfectly," he admitted with a nod.

It did not take long before interrogation revealed the location of the main hideout.

"Tomorrow morning, our next operation begins," Surya said.

Back at the hotel, Sugata turned to Surya and exclaimed, "I'm still amazed—how do you always know so much beforehand?"

Krishna laughed and said, "Nothing now. Everything will be revealed at the very end."

"Alright then... I'll wait."

The next morning, Krishna stretched and grinned. "It looks like today is going to be another thrilling day."

"Let's see," Surya replied. "But first, let's have breakfast."

"Here, you will get nothing but idlis and dosas," said Krishna.

"Sometimes, something different might be nice," said Surya.

Once breakfast was over, they set out again.

• • •

The car stopped in front of a shining, clean, modern house. A man opened the door as the bell rang.

"Veerappa told us to come," Surya said.

"Please come in," the man replied, showing them to a spacious and tastefully decorated drawing room.

Soon, a gentleman entered.

"I hear Veerappa sent you," he said.

"Yes. And if I'm not mistaken, you are the famous art dealer, Mr. Nagaraj?"

"Yes, I am. What brings you here?" He was stiff in manner, but his English was polished and confident.

Surya began, "My friend here is an art collector. His house back in Kolkata is full of rare pieces. When Veerappa heard of his interest, he insisted we meet you. He said your private collection is quite extraordinary."

Nagaraj eyed them doubtfully.

"You could have found plenty in my showroom. Why have you come to my house?"

"Not everything is available in the showroom," Surya replied calmly. "The special pieces are usually kept at home. That's why we came. Right, Sugata?"

"Exactly," Sugata agreed.

"What type of object are you looking for?" asked Nagaraj.

"An exquisite old idol of Vishnu—something striking, unforgettable," Surya said.

"I do have such a piece. Let me show you," said Nagaraj.

Surya said suddenly, "Sugata, why don't you take a look at that Nataraj figure on the corner table?"

Sugata and Krishna walked over. Nagaraj followed, saying, "This is rare and very expensive."

"Cost is not a concern. May I see it more closely?"

"Certainly."

In the meantime, Surya slipped deeper into the house, pistol in hand. In the corridor, he ran into the man who had opened the door earlier.

"Don't move. You see what I'm holding. Take me to Nagaraj's bedroom."

The man understood Hindi, nodded silently, and led him upstairs. Entering the bedroom, Surya locked the door inside.

"Sit quietly. If you make any movement, you're dead."

He scanned the room. If the information was correct, everything was hidden there. One wall held a large Belgian-glass mirror. Surya tugged at it—it swung open like a concealed door, revealing another room. Inside were rows of packing crates. Surya tore open one of the small packets inside, and a puff of fine white powder spilled out.

"Got it."

He locked the man inside and headed back downstairs.

"Where has your friend disappeared?" Nagaraj demanded.

Sugata shrugged. "Who knows? He's unpredictable. He wanders around without warning."

Alarmed, Nagaraj rushed toward the inner rooms. Not finding Surya downstairs, he began climbing the stairs—just as Surya descended.

"How dare you enter my room without permission? I can have you arrested!" Nagaraj shouted furiously.

"The police are already outside. Sugata—call them in," Surya said calmly.

Sugata signalled the four waiting officers.

"What's going on?" Nagaraj cried.

"A walk upstairs will explain everything," Surya replied, "There is a secret room attached to your bedroom, stocked with a large supply of narcotics. We have enough evidence to prove you are one of the major players in this racket."

Nagaraj froze, speechless. The police followed Surya upstairs. The man locked inside was pounding the door and shouting, but one stern warning silenced him. Surya opened the mirror-door, revealing the crates and packets.

"Do you have anything more to say?" Surya asked quietly.

Nagaraj had no answer.

Sugata turned to Surya in admiration and said, "If you hadn't gone in on your own, we would never have discovered this. Incredible intelligence—and courage."

"We had no idea that the drug operations had been running here for so long!" Police Officer Mr. Ramamurthy exclaimed in disbelief.

Nagaraj was arrested, and all the materials were seized.

"Our work here is done," Sugata said. "Let's return to the hotel."

Back at the hotel, the three of them enjoyed a hearty meal—a well-earned celebration of their success.

• • •

Later, the three of them gathered in Krishna's room.

"So it all comes down to drugs," Krishna said quietly. "Now start from the beginning. Tell us everything."

"Alright," Surya replied.

"In the ruins of that old palace in Jhargram, I found a packet of white powder. I knew instantly it was drugs. I also found a phone—probably why they ambushed us later, desperate to get it back."

"So that's why they were so determined to retrieve the phone!" Krishna exclaimed.

"Exactly. From the phone, we gathered plenty of information. The man who was murdered was part of their syndicate. But after a fallout, someone from inside the group took him out. And when we stumbled onto the scene by accident, they shifted the body.

"We tracked one of their bases in Garia through that phone. We went there with the police, but had to pull out almost immediately."

"Why?"

"They knew we were coming. The entire place was rigged with a timed explosive. I spotted the trigger just in time and pulled everyone out. Before leaving, I managed to slip a small notebook into my pocket. Moments after we escaped, the building blew apart."

"Horrifying!" Krishna shuddered. "If you hadn't seen it..."

"Occupational hazard," Surya said calmly. "That notebook gave us new leads—another hub in Diamond Harbour. We didn't know the exact location, so I used Raja, one of my best informers. He stayed undercover and collected everything. Then we moved in. Sugata was with me."

"Yes," Sugata nodded. "But at that time, I had no idea what was really going on. I only learned afterwards."

"From that raid, we seized more drugs—and a laptop. Interrogations and data on the laptop revealed that their Indian bases were in Lucknow and Bengaluru. I had already suspected it, and I knew those areas well."

"That's why you always knew exactly where to look," Sugata said.

"I even know Bangkok is their global headquarters," Surya continued. "After meeting Pankajbabu that day, someone brushed past me on the street and warned me to back off. That's when I realised they were watching. So when I heard about the Purulia trip, I used it as a chance to disappear for a while. Once I returned, we headed for Lucknow. The rest, you already know."

"You're incredible," Krishna said, eyes filled with admiration.

"None of this would've come to light without you," Sugata added.

"If anyone deserves credit, it's Krishna. He's the one who discovered the body in Jhargram. That's where everything started."

Surya stretched. "Alright. We're exhausted. Let's call it a night. Tomorrow, we will explore Bengaluru."

They wished each other good night and drifted back to their rooms, the weight of the revelations still hanging heavily in the air.

• • •

Bengaluru is a beautifully planned city with plenty to see. Cubbon Park was their first stop—vast, green, dense with trees, and dotted with statues of notable personalities. Next, they visited Bangalore Palace—magnificent, modelled after Windsor Castle in England, surrounded by gardens and adorned with exquisite architecture.

Then came the ancient Chola temples, nearly fifteen hundred years old. The intricate craftsmanship left Krishna speechless. They also visited the ISKCON temple.

After that, they reached Tipu Sultan's Summer Palace. Built in a fusion of Hindu and Islamic architectural styles, construction had begun during Hyder Ali's reign and was completed under Tipu Sultan. The result was stunning.

Their tour continued to Lalbagh Botanical Garden, home to a diverse array of plant species. Like the city itself, the garden carried layers of history—from the times of Hyder Ali and Tipu Sultan to the British era and modern independent India.

They stopped for lunch before continuing their sightseeing.

"For today, let's end here," Sugata said, leaning back.

"Let's have a cup of coffee first. The brew here is famous," Surya suggested.

"After this, are we heading straight back to Kolkata?" Krishna asked.

"From here, we can go to Mysore and then to Ooty. I've heard both are beautiful places. Many people take this route. I've been to Bengaluru before, but never had the time to explore. So I was wondering—if we could go, that is, unless anyone has objections," Sugata said.

"Objection? Why on earth?" Krishna laughed, looking at Surya.

"No problem at all," Surya nodded.

And so, the journey to Mysore began.

Mysore—also known as Mahisur or Maishuru—is one of Karnataka's most elegant cities, once the capital of the princely state of Mysore. With its palaces, sandalwood, silks, and spices, the city sits gracefully at the foothills of the Chamundi Hills. After checking in and dining at the hotel, they set out again.

"We'll see the Mysore Palace tomorrow," Surya said.

They drove up the Chamundi Hills. From there, the landscape stretched out below in all directions. The Chamundeshwari Temple stood atop the hill, along with statues of Mahishasura and Nandi.

"The Dussehra festival here is very famous. And the South Kumbh Mela is also held in Mysore," Surya informed them.

"Thanks to Google, you know everything now," Krishna teased.

• • •

Their next stop was the Mysore Zoo—Sri Chamarajendra Zoological Gardens—vast, emerald, and unsettlingly calm, as though hiding secrets behind its pristine enclosures.

By evening, they reached the legendary Brindavan Gardens beside the Krishnaraja Sagar Dam, where the Kaveri flowed in steady, silent darkness.

Under the night sky, the illuminated fountains burst to life, shifting colours across the mist like coded signals.

"The musical fountain show is extraordinary," Sugata murmured, his eyes fixed on the dancing lights.

Over dinner, he added with a grin, "You've managed to solve mysteries and tour half of India at the same time."

"That's how our life runs," Surya chuckled.

"Next, we focus on tracking down their main hideout," Krishna said, his tone turning sharp.

"Oh, still on the case? Try enjoying the view for a minute," Surya teased.

"Exactly," Sugata agreed.

• • •

The next morning, they visited the Mysore Palace—also known as Amba Vilas Palace. Not very ancient, it was built in 1912, blending Hindu, Muslim, Gothic, and Rajput architectural styles. The famed light-and-sound show and the Dussehra festivities have made it world-famous.

It took them a long time to explore the interiors.

"Magnificent!" Surya exclaimed.

"The craftsmanship is unbelievable," Krishna agreed.

Huge, meticulously landscaped gardens stretched around the palace.

"Mysore has many palaces—it's called the 'City of Palaces' for a reason," Surya remarked.

They also visited the Jaganmohan Palace, now home to an art gallery and auditorium. The gallery held exquisite paintings.

"Look carefully, Krishna—you're an artist yourself," Surya nudged him.

"Is he now?" Sugata smiled.

"Oh yes," Surya confirmed. "He paints and does photography. He's even won prizes."

"Well, well—quite a talented man!"

Krishna bought a pair of finely carved sandalwood elephants before lunch. Then they set off for Ooty.

"We'll go through Mudumalai Forest," Surya explained.

"Great!" Krishna said.

This national park lies on the Tamil Nadu–Karnataka border in the Nilgiris and is home to elephants, leopards, tigers, gaur, deer, and many more animals. As their car drove between dense forests, nature seemed to enfold them—green, alive, mysterious.

"Look! A deer just crossed," Krishna pointed out.

"Yes, you can see many animals on this road."

Surya told the driver to be cautious so that no creature would be harmed.

"This was once the domain of the infamous sandalwood bandit Veerappan. People trembled at his name. Eventually, he was hunted down by the police," Sugata said.

"In a place as beautiful as this, violence and bloodshed feel so out of place," Surya sighed.

Just then, Surya received a video call from Ujjayini.

"Where are you now?"

"Driving through Mudumalai Forest, heading from Mysore to Ooty."

"Wow! Show me!"

Surya angled the phone to reveal the thick green forest.

"Amazing—I can even hear the birds!"

"Is there a waterfall nearby?" Surya asked the driver.

"Yes, I'll take you there," he promised.

Soon the sparkling waterfall came into view—a wonderful sight, its foaming water framed by the deep forest.

As evening fell, they reached Ooty—a hill station in Tamil Nadu built during the British era. The cool air hit them pleasantly.

"I like the cold," Krishna said.

Their hotel was beautifully decorated, filled with sculptures, masks, and artistic touches.

• • •

The next day, their Ooty tour began at Doddabetta Peak—the highest point of the Nilgiri range, complete with a telescope observatory.

"Look at the view; it's breathtaking," Sugata whispered.

From there, they headed to the Kalhatti Waterfalls near Kalhatti village, a place associated with Sage Agastya and popular among birdwatchers.

Next, they enjoyed boating on Ooty Lake, surrounded by neat shops and lush greenery.

They later explored the Ooty Botanical Garden—well-maintained, diverse, and home to rare plants, including a fossilised tree trunk believed to be 20 million years old.

"There are so many varieties!" Krishna exclaimed.

"He loves plants—has a beautiful rooftop garden at home," Surya told Sugata.

"No end to his talents!" Sugata laughed.

By evening, they returned to rest.

The next morning, they toured the renowned Nilgiri tea factory, watching the tea-processing steps and buying various blends, including cardamom tea and chocolate tea.

They also visited the Deer Park, home to sambars and chital. Naturally, they stocked up on chocolates—the region is famous for them.

After days of wandering, Surya finally said, "Now, it's time to go back to Kolkata."

"And after that, Bangkok again," Krishna added.

"Yes—first let's get home," Surya replied.

• • •

But the moment they returned to Kolkata, trouble struck hard.

Krishna went down with a fierce fever. Dr. Samaddar examined him, and though the medicines brought the temperature down, Krishna remained drained and weak.

"Take two days of rest—you'll be fine," Ujjayini said softly.

Krishna managed a weary smile.

"Too much travelling. Your body couldn't keep up," Surya muttered as he set down a packet. "I brought grapes and sweets—your favourites."

"But Bangkok is still pending…" Krishna sighed.

"We'll see. First, get well," Surya replied.

"Then we'll celebrate properly!" Ujjayini added.

Meanwhile, Mohit Bajpai flew in from Delhi and met Surya in private.

"You've carried this case from the start," he said. "Only you can finish the final operation in Bangkok. You have to go—and Sugata Ray must accompany you."

The Chief's voice grew firm, almost solemn. "You've brought the mission this far, Surya. But the last step has to be completed by you. Sugata will go with you—he's seasoned, and you work well together."

Surya nodded slowly. "Alright. I'll go."

"Good. All arrangements will be ready in a couple of days."

But for days now, Surya had sensed it—that faint prickle at the back of his neck, the shadow that never quite disappeared. Someone was following him. Watching him. He would have to stay alert.

He was riding in the front seat of a police jeep, the vehicle inching through heavy traffic, when it happened.

A sudden blast tore through the street. Fire engulfed the jeep in seconds.

And Surya was gone.

• • •

A heavy pall of grief settled over everyone. A brilliant, unwavering investigator—one who had spent his life serving the nation—had met a brutal end. The news spread like wildfire.

The entire police force was shaken. With a grim heart, Sugata went to break the news to Krishna.

Krishna was lying on his bed, reading a book, his strength mostly restored. At the sound of the doorbell, he rose and opened the door.

"Oh—Sugatada! Please, come in."

Sugata stepped inside and sat down without a word.

"What happened? You look... devastated," Krishna said, unease creeping into his voice.

"There's terrible news."

"Terrible? What happened?" Krishna stood up, tension tightening his posture.

"Your Suryada... he's gone."

"Gone? What do you mean?"

Sugata told him everything.

Krishna collapsed into his chair, as though the floor had vanished beneath him. Words deserted him. When he finally managed to speak, he called Sreeja and Ujjayini, who rushed over immediately. The room was swallowed by a stunned, suffocating silence—no one could find the strength to console another.

"This is why I begged him not to dig so deep into crime syndicates," Ujjayini whispered, tears streaming down her face. "Look how it ended."

• • •

The next morning, Sugata returned to Krishna, rested a hand on his shoulder, and said gently, "What has happened can't be undone. But our duty isn't over. Come with me to

Bangkok—we'll finish what he started. We'll end this cartel once and for all."

"No. I can't go, not without Suryada." Krishna's voice trembled, his eyes wet.

"Don't you want his mission fulfilled? If we crush these monsters, that will be your loyalty—your love—for him."

Krishna stared at the floor for a long moment, and then nodded. "Alright. I'll go to Bangkok."

• • •

News of Surya's death dominated every newspaper and television channel. Debate panels sprang up, and investigators quickly began pointing toward the drug cartel.

Krishna and Sugata reached the airport. Surya's memories surged through Krishna, tightening in his throat like a vice. Sugata gripped his shoulder, urging him to stay strong.

Both men looked different now—moustaches, beards, glasses—just enough to slip past recognition.

On the plane, Krishna stared out of the window, a silent wish echoing in his mind: *If only Suryada could return by some miracle.*

Bangkok's Suvarnabhumi Airport—*the Land of Gold*—lay shimmering under the afternoon light.

At the hotel, they inserted local SIM cards.

"I'm stepping out to meet the police here," Sugata said before heading out.

Krishna, drained by everything weighing on his mind, fell asleep almost instantly.

Hours later, Sugata returned; the discussions were complete.

After dinner in the hotel lounge, they retired for the night. Sugata drifted off immediately, but Krishna remained awake, standing by the window, watching the glowing avenues below.

Bangkok, once known as Siam, is bordered by Myanmar, Laos, and Cambodia.

• • •

The next morning, Sugata said quietly, "The operation goes down this evening."

They spent the day moving from place to place, pretending to be tourists, but Krishna's mind never left the mission.

By 6 p.m., both were dressed and ready. Sugata slipped a gun into Krishna's hand. "Keep this. You may need it."

Their vehicle stopped in front of a tall, nondescript building.

"It's showtime," Sugata murmured.

Four local officers joined them at the entrance. Together, they rode the elevator to the seventh floor. A sign read: **The Royal Flavours**.

Sugata pressed the bell.

A man opened the door.

"Appointment. Code—Yellow Dragon," Sugata said.

They were ushered inside and seated. Moments later, another man walked in—sharp-eyed, coiled with authority. He was the boss.

"Where are you from?" he asked.

"India."

"And him?" He gestured toward one of the officers.

"He's local and trusted."

"So what do you want?"

"Business," Sugata replied coolly.

"What business?"

"Drugs."

The boss burst into laughter.

On cue, four armed guards stormed in, grabbing Sugata and Krishna, binding their hands, stripping them of their phones and weapons. One of the phones was still recording.

"So you thought you could trap me?" the boss sneered. "Pathetic. I know this officer, local police. And in India, someone named Surya shut down all our channels. I hear everything. Before he reached my Bangkok network, I blew up his car."

"You killed Suryada? You monster!" Krishna shouted.

"Yes," the boss said, lifting his gun toward Krishna. "And now all of you will die. Your bodies will float down the river by morning."

A voice cut through the tension.

"And where will *you* go?"

Everyone froze.

Krishna looked up—and the air left his lungs.

Surya stood there, alive.

Before the boss could react, Surya lunged, knocking him aside and disarming him in one fluid motion. Police officers stormed the room, subduing the guards.

"Game over," Surya said as he untied Krishna and Sugata.

Shock, relief, disbelief—everything crashed into Krishna at once. He grabbed Surya's shoulders. "You… you *are* Suryada!"

"Of course," Surya grinned. "One hundred percent original. No dramatic twin brothers." He chuckled. "I'll explain later. For now, let's wrap this up."

A massive stash of drugs was seized, and the men were arrested.

"This is only one layer," Surya said. "There's someone above him."

"Where are we going now?" Sugata asked.

"Bangkok Night Market," Surya replied.

"What? For shopping?" Krishna blurted.

"That too," Surya said with a faint smile. "But first—the real business."

• • •

The night market throbbed with neon and noise, the crowd a shifting sea of shadows. At a cramped clothing stall, Surya murmured, "Here…"

In a heartbeat, the officer sealed off the area, whispered something to the trembling shop owner, and followed a worker down a narrow stairway. Surya, Krishna, and Sugata slipped in behind them.

Fear had already broken the owner; the truth spilt out of him like a burst dam.

Below, the basement opened into a hidden labyrinth stacked with packets of drugs—an underground nerve centre where the entire cartel operated. At its heart sat the kingpin, relaxed and smug, certain his empire was untouchable.

"From Jhargram to Bangkok... the full circle," Surya said quietly. "Now this network finally comes to an end."

The takedown that followed was fast, precise, and merciless.

• • •

Back at the hotel, a separate room had already been arranged for Surya.

"Now tell us everything," Krishna demanded.

"In Kolkata," Surya began, his voice low, "the cartel had decided I wouldn't make it to Bangkok—at least not alive. We discovered a bomb planted in the car assigned to me. Seconds before ignition, the driver and I switched to another vehicle and sped away. The blast tore the first car apart. The area had been cleared in advance, and news of my 'death' spread instantly. I needed the cartel to believe I was gone. Krishna, Sreeja, Ujjayini... I knew the lie would break their hearts, but it was the only way."

He continued, "I came here in disguise, gathered information, and made sure I was close enough to watch over you during the raid. I even secured duplicate keys so I could slip inside before anyone else."

Krishna let out a laugh. "What an entrance—like the hero of some action movie!"

"And without you, we'd have been dead," Sugata said, shaking his head.

Calls were made to Sreeja and Ujjayini. Once the truth was revealed, Sreeja was overwhelmed.

"You scared us half to death! Now be careful—and come home soon. When you return, you're coming straight to our place," Ujjayini insisted.

Tiyasha chimed in, "Mamu, when you come back, I want to hear the entire story."

"I always knew nothing could truly harm you," Ujjayini added, her relief unmistakable.

Sugata also spoke with Mr. Vajpayee, who congratulated Surya for the operation's success.

Later, when things had quieted, Krishna leaned toward Sugata. "Did you know about any of this?"

"Not at all," Sugata replied.

"Only a select few did," Surya said with a faint smile.

"Tomorrow, we tour Bangkok," Krishna said, a spark of excitement returning to his voice.

• • •

Pattaya is a coastal city in Thailand, known for its famous beaches.

"Many people are enjoying water sports," said Sugata, standing on Pattaya Beach.

Krishna rode a water bike for a while, and Surya went parasailing. They also viewed corals through a glass-bottom boat.

Next, they visited the Sanctuary of Truth—a magnificent structure made entirely of teak wood. It is neither a temple nor a palace, yet it looks like a blend of both. Built by a prominent local businessman, it stands as a symbol of art, culture, and philosophy. The intricate sculptures inside are breathtaking.

Then they went to Wat Phra Khao Yai, or Big Buddha Hill, where a huge golden statue of Buddha towers over the area. It is also a temple, visited by many who come to pray.

"Look, there are many small Buddha statues too," Krishna pointed out. After leaving the place, Surya said, "That's enough sightseeing for today."

The next morning, they visited the Nong Nooch Tropical Garden, a beautiful place filled with various species of butterflies, plants, and flowers. Cultural shows are held here, and there is also a restaurant. They stopped by Art in Paradise, an art gallery featuring three-dimensional paintings.

"Look at these 3D artworks," Surya told Krishna.

"Yes, amazing! Great concept," Krishna replied.

After Pattaya, they planned to go to Phuket, a world-famous scenic destination in southern Thailand. The island is a major attraction for tourists, known for its beautiful beaches, and is Thailand's largest island. "I don't like the food here," said Sugata.

"Me neither," Krishna agreed.

They visited Patong Beach. "So many people everywhere—so lively!" Surya remarked. "Phuket is famous for its natural beauty," Sugata added. They explored Phuket Town, where the strong Chinese influence was noticeable in the museums and art galleries. They also went on an island boat tour.

"This is a tremendous experience," said Sugata.

"Let's go to James Bond Rocks now," Surya suggested.

"Yes, we must see that," Krishna replied eagerly.

The next day, they visited the Phuket Big Buddha, a huge white jade statue atop Nakkerd Hill.

"The place feels very peaceful," Surya said, as the sound of bells echoed around them. Later, they visited the Wat Chalong Pagoda, where Buddha's relics are preserved. Inside were wax statues of two revered Buddhist monks.

"Look, the murals depict the life of Gautama Buddha," Krishna noted. "There are many golden Buddha statues here, too," Surya added.

Their next stop was the Gibbon Rehabilitation Centre, where trafficked gibbons are rescued and rehabilitated. Visitors may even get a chance to see them in the surrounding forest.

"They are doing wonderful work here," said Surya.

"Right. Look there," Krishna pointed.

The guide explained that gibbons are small apes, while gorillas, orangutans, and chimpanzees are great apes found in the forests of Southeast Asia.

From there, they trekked through the forest to a waterfall and later visited the Phuket Museum, which also features a 3D art gallery. "So you've seen plenty of photos, then?" Surya asked.

"Yes, quite enough," Krishna replied.

Back at the hotel, Surya spoke on the phone for a while.

"Bangkok is done. Now it's time to return to Kolkata," Krishna said.

"Not Kolkata—we'll go to Delhi first," Surya replied.

"Why Delhi? Do you have some work there?" Krishna asked.

"Yes. A Serious work. Want to hear what it is?" Surya said.

"If you tell me, I'll listen," Krishna responded.

"Then listen," Surya began. "I went through their laptops and mobiles and found they're connected to an extremist organization. After further searching, I discovered their next plan—and it's extremely dangerous. Next week, the India Festival is happening in Delhi. Many guests and artists from India and abroad will attend. Representatives from several countries will be present. It's a huge event. They've planned a bombing there."

"This is terrible!" exclaimed Sugata. "This must be stopped."

"As soon as I found out, I informed Mr. Vajpayee. He informed Delhi. Then Vikas Goel from Delhi contacted me and asked me to come. That's why I'm going."

The three remained silent for a while. Finally, Krishna said, "But I must return to Kolkata. I'll stay updated over the phone." Surya nodded. "Fine. What else can be done? But I want to tell you one thing—if you don't mind."

"Yes, go ahead."

"No one else should know about this matter. I'm sure you're in serious danger."

"Don't worry. I won't tell anyone."

Just then, Ujjayini called. "So, the Bangkok trip is over. Now it's time to return to Kolkata."

"Before that, we have to go to Delhi once."

"Again Delhi? You've already been there."

"Yes, have to go there once more."

"Hmm… is it only for sightseeing? *Dal mein kuch kala hai.*"

"I won't say anything now—you'll hear it later."

Surya spoke again with Mr. Goel.

• • •

Surya and Krishna landed at the Delhi airport. A man holding a placard was waiting for them. He escorted them to a car, and after a short drive, it stopped in front of a small house.

"You'll be staying here," he said.

Krishna looked suspiciously. "We're not staying in a hotel?"

"No," Surya replied. "Mr. Goel and I discussed it. This is to maintain secrecy."

The house was neatly arranged. After a while, Mr. Goel arrived.

"Do you like the place?" he asked.

"Yes, very much. You've arranged everything nicely."

"Good. A bodyguard will stay with you. That's very important."

"We have to act quickly. The event is in two days. The bomb squad has scanned the entire area but found nothing. You should visit the venue once."

"Of course, I will."

"Alright, take some rest."

"Can the event be cancelled?" Krishna asked.

"Impossible. We tried, but it didn't work."

"Okay... nothing else to do then."

Surya, Krishna, and their bodyguard headed to the event venue. The bodyguard's name was Vishal.

Surya inspected the entire building. It was large and heavily secured. Mr. Goel introduced him to the security in charge, Ramesh Sharma.

After stepping outside, Mr. Goel asked, "What do you think, Mr. Chatterjee?"

"We haven't found anything suspicious yet," Surya said. "Let's see."

Back at the house, Surya listened to music on his phone while Krishna switched on the TV.

During dinner, Surya said, "Krishna, this time it's a tough challenge."

"That's nothing. If you're here, everything will be fine."

"You sure?"

"Yes, one hundred per cent."

Surya and Krishna stayed on the first floor, while Vishal occupied the ground floor. Vishal was a quiet man.

That evening, Surya sat deep in thought. The event would begin the next day, and he planned to leave early for the venue. Krishna had gone to bed, and Vishal was downstairs. Surya went up to the terrace. The terrace always filled him with a special kind of energy. A crescent moon hung in the sky, clouds drifting softly around it. His mind felt lighter there.

The next morning, Krishna said, "Suryada, don't stress too much. Everything will be fine."

Surya smiled. "Thank you. You're always by my side."

Slowly, people began gathering at the venue. Surya spoke briefly with Ramesh.

"Everyone is on alert. No worries," Ramesh said.

"Okay."

The event was scheduled for 2 p.m. The India Festival was extremely important; everyone's eyes would be on it.

Mr. Goel arrived as well.

"With you here, I hope nothing unfortunate will happen," he said.

Surya only smiled faintly.

"You look around everywhere. If you spot anything suspicious, inform me immediately," Surya told Krishna.

"Alright."

Surya kept checking the CCTV cameras from time to time. Suddenly, he noticed that the two security guards at the south gate were asleep. It was highly unusual. He called Ramesh. Even after shaking them, the guards didn't wake up. They were in deep sleep.

"It looks like a strong dose of sleeping medicine," Surya said.

"Who gave them sleeping pills?" Ramesh asked.

"We'll have to find out. Come, let's check the CCTV footage."

As they examined the footage, the truth became clear. Someone had approached the guards and offered them sherbet. Minutes later, the guards fell asleep. Immediately after that, four men entered, each carrying a suitcase. They walked straight into the auditorium.

"At that time, I had gone to speak with Mr. Goel. I'd told Vishal to watch," Surya said.

Vishal added quietly, "Sir… I was on a phone call at that moment."

Ramesh scolded him sharply.

"Fine, what's done is done. Let's get to the auditorium quickly," Surya said, moving swiftly with Ramesh.

• • •

The event was already underway, the auditorium packed to the last seat.

"All guards stay alert. No one is to eat or drink anything," Surya instructed Ramesh sharply.

"And the new guards at the side gate?"

"Posted. Everything is covered."

"Good."

Surya had a grim suspicion about the contents of those suitcases. The enemy's plan was unfolding with chilling precision, and a major threat loomed ahead.

Just as Surya and Ramesh approached, the auditorium doors slammed shut.

Krishna was inside. He had noticed the four men with suitcases earlier, but dismissed them as staff. Then, without warning, three men slipped into different corners of the hall. The fourth bolted onto the stage—where dignitaries were seated, and music filled the air—pulled out a gun, and shouted:

"Don't move! One wrong move and everyone dies! Four powerful bombs have been planted in this auditorium. They'll go off right on time. My men have already placed them. Now the real game begins!"

The other three drew guns as well. They shoved the security personnel outside and sealed the doors. The guards, terrified that resistance might trigger chaos, backed down.

"Why are you doing this?" Raghunath Tripathi demanded from the stage.

"Are you terrorists?" Sudip Samanta called out from the audience.

"Exactly!" the gunman on stage roared with a mocking laugh.

"What did we ever do to you? Let us go!" someone pleaded.

"Shut up! One more word and you're dead!" another gunman barked.

A suffocating silence fell over the hall.

Krishna slipped into a corner and quietly called Surya.

"I'm watching everything on CCTV," Surya said. "Hang up. Stay alert."

"Alright."

"These men are ruthless. No mistakes."

"What do you want from us?" Tripathi asked.

"For now? Money. Fifty million dollars," the leader said. "Give us the cash and a way out. No tricks."

Krishna stepped forward. "My elder brother is outside. He has government connections. He can convey your demands."

"Good. Call him. I'll speak to him myself."

Krishna dialed Surya and handed over the phone.

"We want fifty million dollars and a safe escape," the leader announced. "A helicopter. We will fly straight to Dubai. You have five hours. Fail, and everyone dies."

"But you'll die too," Surya warned.

"Not your concern. We're not afraid of death. Stop wasting time."

"Fifty million isn't easy to arrange—"

"No more talking! Tell us when it's ready."

He cut the call.

The situation was spiraling into a nightmare. Surya briefed Mr. Goel, who relayed everything to the authorities. Minutes later, the Home Minister called.

"I've heard the details," he said gravely. "We may have no choice but to agree. Too many lives are at stake."

"But even if we agree, there's no guarantee they'll keep their word," Surya argued. "And giving in will only fuel more terrorism. Maybe there's another way—"

"No. We can't risk lives. Tell them we accept and are working on it."

"...Alright."

Surya's heart sank, but he knew the game wasn't over. Not yet.

He called the gang leader. "The government has agreed."

"Good. Finally. Tell them to hurry."

"Just make sure no one gets hurt."

The line went dead.

• • •

Inside, an elderly man weakly asked for a glass of water.

"Shall I bring him some?" Krishna whispered.

"No," the leader snapped. "No one leaves their place."

Krishna fell silent. No one dared to guess what these men might do next. Fear had sunk its claws into every corner of the auditorium.

The Home Minister had already arrived, and Surya stayed glued to his side, the pressure mounting with each passing second.

Without warning, Surya slipped away toward the back of the auditorium. A few minutes later, he returned with a spark in his eyes.

"I've found a way," he murmured.

"What way?" Vishal asked.

"I'll explain later. Go to the Home Minister and keep him from coming here."

"Alright," Vishal said, hurrying off.

Behind the auditorium was a small door, locked from the outside. Surya decided that would be his entry point. He sent a message to Krishna: *I'm going in from the back.*

Okay, Krishna replied, positioning himself to monitor the dimly lit doorway.

Moments later, Surya slipped inside. Krishna moved toward one of the terrorists, giving him a casual signal. As the man approached, Krishna suddenly turned his phone's volume up—blasting a loud Hindi song. In that burst of noise, Surya clamped a hand over the terrorist's mouth and shot him cleanly through the chest with a silenced pistol. The muffled sound vanished under the music. Surya dragged the body out; Krishna quietly took the man's place.

"Who's playing music at full volume?" the leader barked.

"I am," Krishna replied coolly. "Feeling tense… thought I'd listen to something."

"Tense? Don't worry, all your tension will end soon. Turn it off."

Krishna obeyed—and felt his phone buzz again. Surya was calling.

"Listen," Surya whispered, "give the leader your phone. Tell him the government wants to talk. While he's distracted, get behind him. Take his gun if you can. Once you've got him under control, I'll come in. We can't afford a mistake."

"Okay, boss."

"What's taking you so long on that call?" the leader demanded.

"The government is calling," Krishna said. "They want to speak with you. They've accepted your demands…"

A slow, smug smile curled across the leader's face. "I knew it. They all are cowards."

Grinding his teeth, Krishna handed him the phone. As the leader started speaking, Krishna slipped behind him, pressed a gun into his back, and snatched his weapon away.

"Move and you're dead," Krishna growled. "Now you'll see who the real coward is—the one sneaking around like a thief."

The leader froze, stunned. He hadn't anticipated this.

Surya burst in with four commandos. The remaining two terrorists lunged for their guns, but Surya's team dropped them before they could fire. When the leader tried to shove Krishna away, Krishna put him down and pinned him to the floor.

"Well done, Krishna!" Surya shouted.

Krishna struck the leader hard across the face. "You wouldn't even give an old man water. Heartless devil!"

"He'll get what he deserves," Surya said. "Right now, we need to find the bombs."

The bomb squad rushed inside as the leader was handcuffed. Surya, Krishna, and the commandos escorted the hostages out.

"Clear the area immediately," Surya ordered.

The bombs were found and defused just in time. Outside, relatives clung to their loved ones, relief spreading across their faces.

"We're safe," Krishna said, exhaling. "Your plan worked."

"You played your part perfectly," Surya replied.

People pointed toward Surya's team. "Because of them, we're alive!"

"There's still work to do," Surya said, heading back inside. Krishna followed.

Surya turned to Ramesh. "Did you find the person who gave drugged sherbet to the guards?"

"Yes—there he is."

"Good. We need to know their next move. The leader won't talk."

The Home Minister arrived, clapping Surya on the back. "Well done."

"Apologies for acting without informing you, sir," Surya said. "But we couldn't afford to wait."

"You're a hero, Surya."

"Let's interrogate him," Commissioner Malhotra said. But the suspect refused to speak.

"We'll make him talk at the station. Bring him."

The entire team headed to the police station, while media channels lit up with praise for Surya and his men.

A call came from Ujjayini, her voice heavy with worry. "What happened? Are you safe?"

"Yes. Everything's under control. The country narrowly avoided a disaster," Surya said.

"That's because of you. I knew something was off the moment you left for Delhi. I saw the news—your face was everywhere. Tell me everything later. Congratulations!"

"Thank you."

Then his sister Srija called. "Another stunt? I'm proud of you—but terrified. Come home soon."

"Okay, didi. I'll call later."

"Take care."

"We should head back," Surya sighed. "I'm exhausted."

"Same here," Krishna replied.

After some coffee and a hot meal, they finally felt their nerves settling.

"You're all heroes now," Vishal said with a grin.

Soon, they drifted into a deep, much-needed sleep.

• • •

Naturally, they woke up late the next morning. Surya's phone began to ring, slicing through the quiet.

"Who's calling now?" he muttered.

"Mr. Malhotra," Krishna replied.

"Give it to me."

Surya held the phone to his ear. "Good morning."

"Good morning," Malhotra said. "None of them has spoken yet."

"Keep trying," Surya said, his voice steady. The call ended with a click.

After breakfast, Surya dialled Mr. Goel. "Please arrange our return to Kolkata."

"Of course," Goel replied. "And check today's newspapers—you're everywhere, photos and all. Outstanding work."

When the line went dead, Surya picked up another phone.

"Whose phone is that?" Krishna asked.

"Guess."

"…the leader's?"

"Correct."

"Looking for something?"

"Yes. Let's see what secrets he left behind."

Krishna began scrolling through his own phone while Surya dug into the device. Moments later, Goel called again.

"All arrangements for your departure are complete," he said.

"Thank you," Surya replied.

"You're welcome. And one more thing—the two terrorists who tried to escape were shot dead by the police."

"Oh. Alright."

Surya relayed the news to Krishna.

"Encounter?" Krishna asked.

"Yes. I figured it would end this way."

"It's better," Krishna said quietly. "If they'd stayed alive, their people would've kidnapped someone… maybe even hijacked a plane."

Surya nodded. "Exactly."

• • •

After returning to Kolkata, the two of them slept deeply, exhaustion finally giving way to clarity. By morning, they felt refreshed.

"Did you find anything new on that phone?" Krishna asked.

"So that's what's been circling in your mind?" Surya replied, eyeing him.

"Yes, please tell me," Krishna said, his voice tight with worry.

"What I found is significant," Surya said at last. "In a week, there's a major international environmental conference in Indonesia. Heads of state from several countries will be present. They're planning something there."

"What? A blast?"

"I don't know yet. But the organisation's commander-in-chief will personally supervise the mission. The one in Delhi was just a deputy."

"That's serious. Won't you inform them?"

"I already did. I've emailed Mr. Goel."

Moments later, the Home Minister called. "You've given us another invaluable information. We've already contacted the Indonesian government. But tell me—can't the seminar be cancelled?"

"At first, I thought so too," Surya said. "But cancelling it will only embolden them. Next time, they'll strike anywhere, anytime. If we can neutralise them there, their entire network will collapse."

"You're absolutely right. I'll convey this to their government as well."

"But there's one more thing," Surya added.

"What is it?"

"You want me to go there myself and foil their plot. No one else, right?"

"Yes. Only you can handle this. I've already spoken to their government—they agreed."

"I'm sorry. I've travelled too much already. I can't do it anymore. Please send someone else."

"Think again, Surya. This concerns national honour."

Krishna turned to him. "They want you to go to Indonesia?"

"Yes, but I refused."

"Alright," Krishna murmured.

Just then, the doorbell rang.

Surya opened the door—and froze for a second. "Gaurav! Come in!"

Gaurav, his childhood friend and a sharp CID officer, stepped in with a grin.

"How are you?" Surya asked.

"I'm fine. And you—always landing one spectacular case after another," Gaurav teased. "Now tell me, what's going on here?"

"What's going on? Can't a man visit his friend?" he laughed. "Right, Krishna? And how's your photography going?"

"It's going well, dada," Krishna replied.

"Good, good. Surya… I actually came for a reason."

"What reason?" Surya asked, already knowing it wouldn't be simple.

"You refused the Indonesia assignment. The Home Ministry still wants you there. And somehow, they discovered you're my friend. They asked me to convince you. So… let's go together."

"No, I can't continue travelling like this."

"Come on—for my sake! And I'll get to see Indonesia," Gaurav added with a mischievous smile.

Surya couldn't help laughing. "Alright, fine—I'll go. You're my friend, and during that first mystery, you helped me more than anyone."

"The tiger mystery!" Krishna chimed in.

"Thank you for agreeing," Gaurav said earnestly.

"Well, happy now? And Krishna—you wanted us to go too, didn't you?"

"Something like that," Krishna admitted.

Kamala arrived with tea and *luchi-tarkari*.

"Ah, *luchi* and *tarkari*! Perfect," Gaurav said, delighted.

Just then, Ujjayini entered the room. "Well, well… looks like a cosy little meeting is happening here."

"Sit, didi. Did you bring something?"

"Yes—chicken kebab."

"Excellent. And listen—we're heading out on another mission."

"Where now?"

"Indonesia."

After hearing everything, Ujjayini said calmly, "Good. But these people are extremely dangerous. You both must be careful."

"We will," Surya assured her.

They handed her a showpiece they'd bought in Thailand, which instantly brightened her face.

Once Gaurav and Ujjayini left, Surya leaned back. "Alright. Let's finish this job too. Indonesia isn't far from Malaysia. Remember when we went to Singapore–Malaysia?"

"How could I forget? That mysterious doll case. That was a tough one," Krishna replied.

• • •

Surya, Krishna, and Gaurav boarded the flight to Indonesia, the weight of the mission pressing down on all three.

One test after another, Surya thought as the aircraft cut through the clouds.

Indonesia—an archipelago of countless islands: Java, Sumatra, Borneo, New Guinea, and Bali. Their destination was Jakarta, where the high-profile conference would take place. Upon landing, a designated contact whisked them away from the airport, driving them to a discreet safe house arranged to keep their arrival secret.

Once inside, Surya dropped onto the sofa, eyes sharp despite the fatigue.

"We have very little time," he said. "Every second counts."

A short while later, Mr. Nair from the Indian Embassy arrived.

"I need to survey the conference venue," Surya said without preamble.

"Let's move," Mr. Nair replied.

At the venue, Surya's gaze swept across every corner, every angle, every possible breach. He spoke to the officer in charge.

"Go through all CCTV footage—frame by frame if needed."

"Our cameras are powerful, sir. They cover a wide range," the officer assured him.

"Good. Pull up today's recordings."

After reviewing the footage for a while, Surya said, "Alright. We'll come again tomorrow."

• • •

The next day, while combing through the CCTV footage yet again, Surya froze.

"That man. We need to follow him—Krishna, now!"

The police chief moved in beside them. On-screen, the man slipped into a car. Surya's team tailed him without hesitation.

Twenty minutes later, the suspect's vehicle halted near a deserted stretch. He and his driver disappeared into a dilapidated old house.

"That's the commander-in-chief of the terrorist organisation," Surya said quietly. "He came to inspect the site. They're planning something big."

"How can you be sure?" Krishna asked.

"From the deputy's mobile we recovered in Delhi."

Surya's eyes were sharp. "Now we plan how to take them down."

"We can storm the place," Krishna suggested.

"No. That could cost lives. We don't know how many operatives he has."

"Surya's right," Gaurav added.

A faint glow flickered inside the structure.

"Look—the light is on," Krishna whispered.

The house stood alone, two storeys high, isolated—chosen with purpose.

Police units arrived and held position at a distance.

"There's a back door," Gaurav said. "Flimsy."

"Good. Break it—quietly," Surya ordered.

One soft shove and the door splintered. A towering figure stood before them, gun raised. The shot grazed past—Surya's bullet answered cleanly, dropping him.

Two more men thundered down the stairs, but Gaurav and Surya cut them down before they could react.

"The commander must be upstairs," Gaurav said.

Surya paused, uneasy. "Something's wrong."

He stepped back outside—and saw the commander descending a rope, sprinting into the darkness.

"Stop!" Surya shouted.

The commander fired wildly as he ran. Krishna took the shot—his bullet struck the fugitive in the back. The man collapsed with a scream.

Inside, no one else remained. Four bodies were found. Operation was over.

"That's it," Surya said calmly. "My job's done. The police can unravel the rest. Come on, Krishna."

"I'll join later. Your car will drop you," Gaurav said.

Surya and Krishna left.

Later, after repeated knocks, Surya finally opened the door for Gaurav.

"We fell asleep," Surya admitted.

"Good. Now let's eat," Gaurav said.

"I'm starving," Krishna added.

Over dinner, Gaurav leaned forward. "They were planning a full-scale explosion. You stopped the entire operation. And now the rest of their network will be rounded up. Their organisation is finished. But how did you identify the commander?"

"The deputy—the one behind the Delhi attack—had his photo on his phone. I recognised him on the CCTV. I knew he'd personally inspect the site. And he did," Surya replied.

"He didn't know a genius was waiting to dismantle his entire plan," Krishna said.

"Well said," Gaurav laughed. "This is why you're the master of detective work."

The Indonesian government honoured Surya's team in a formal ceremony.

Surya called Ujjayini as well.

"Wonderful! With you there, everything turns out right," she said. "Now you'll finally explore Indonesia, won't you?"

"Yes, we will."

"Good. Enjoy. Tell me everything when you return."

Soon after, Mr. Goel called. "Congratulations, Mr. Chatterjee. You've made our country proud."

The Home Minister also called to thank him.

"So," Gaurav grinned at Surya, "Indonesia sightseeing now? No more work left."

"Gladly," Krishna said.

And their tour began.

• • •

Merdeka Square is one of Jakarta's most important landmarks, five times larger than Tiananmen Square in China. At its centre stands the National Monument—a symbol of the city and a monument built to honour Indonesia's freedom struggle. They also visited the Jakarta History Museum, where many ancient artefacts are preserved. Very close to Merdeka Square is the National Museum of Jakarta, whose vast collection can captivate any visitor.

Next, they explored Taman Mini Indonesia Park, a place that offers a fascinating insight into Indonesian culture and history. Traditional houses from across the country stand throughout the park, each representing a unique heritage style. They later visited Jakarta's Chinatown, full of shops, food stalls, and beautiful temples.

After sightseeing and eating, their next destination was Bali. Bali is one of the world's greatest tourist attractions, and the island's beaches are simply breathtaking.

"So finally we've seen the famous Bali," Gaurav said.

"It looks like a painting made by a master artist," Surya added.

They then travelled to Borobudur, the ancient 8th-century Buddhist temple that is now a UNESCO World Heritage Site and one of Java's main attractions. In Borneo, they visited Tanjung Puting National Park to see orangutans.

"These animals are endangered species," Surya said. "This place has the highest population of orangutans in the world."

They also saw the famous Komodo dragons at Komodo National Park. "We've only read about dragons in stories, but today we saw them with our own eyes!" Gaurav said.

"They look terrifying," Krishna added.

The national park consists of several islands, and visitors can take boat rides or go snorkelling there. On Komodo Island, the pink beach is especially famous.

"Look how pink the sand is," Surya said.

Their guide explained that Komodo dragons are venomous and their bite is strong enough to paralyse prey. They can grow up to ten feet long and weigh around 130 kilograms. They hunt various animals and even eat their own kind. In some cases, they have attacked humans as well, and they are powerful enough to bring down an elephant.

Earlier, they had visited Bali's Sacred Monkey Forest in Ubud, the cultural heart of Bali. A special species of monkey lives in this forest, and the Ubud Temple holds great significance. Balinese Hinduism blends aspects of many different religions.

Mount Bromo was another highlight—a volcano whose peak was blown off during an eruption.

"What a beautiful place," Surya said.

"Look, smoke is rising from the top," Gaurav pointed out.

They also visited Lake Toba, formed inside a volcanic crater. It is believed to have been created by a massive eruption nearly seventy thousand years ago. Visitors can enjoy boating, fishing, and swimming there.

"You two have travelled to many countries because of all these investigations," Gaurav said to Krishna.

"Well, yes, we've ended up touring quite a few places," Krishna replied.

• • •

In the evening, Surya told Gaurav, "You sing well, right? Sing something for us."

"Really? Let's do it then!" Gaurav laughed.

"I never knew that!" Krishna exclaimed.

"I used to sing long ago. I haven't practised in years," Gaurav said.

"That won't do. You have to sing."

"Yes, start," Surya insisted.

"Alright, since you won't let me escape," Gaurav said, and began singing Kishore Kumar's song—*'Ei Je Nodi, Jaay Sagore…'*

When he finished, Surya and Krishna said together, "Amazing!"

"What a beautiful voice you have! You must sing more," Krishna said.

Gaurav sang a few more songs. After that, they ate dinner.

"Krishna, aren't you going to draw the Komodo dragon?" Surya asked.

"No way! I'll draw the mountains and lakes instead."

"Much better," Gaurav agreed.

Finally, they returned to Kolkata.

• • •

"No more trips for quite a few days," Surya said.

Two days later, Ujjayini arrived and said, "Come on, let's go buy movie tickets."

"Movie?" Surya asked.

"Yes! Why not? Today is Sunday."

"Of course we're going," Krishna said.

After the movie, they dined at a restaurant.

Seeing the Komodo dragon photo, Ujjayini shivered. Then she said, "Let's go somewhere for a day trip."

"Where?" Krishna asked.

"We can go to the Itachuna Rajbari."

"Another palace?" Surya groaned.

"As long as there's no bloodshed," Krishna joked.

"And even if there is, it'll lead to a new mystery!" Surya added with a grin.